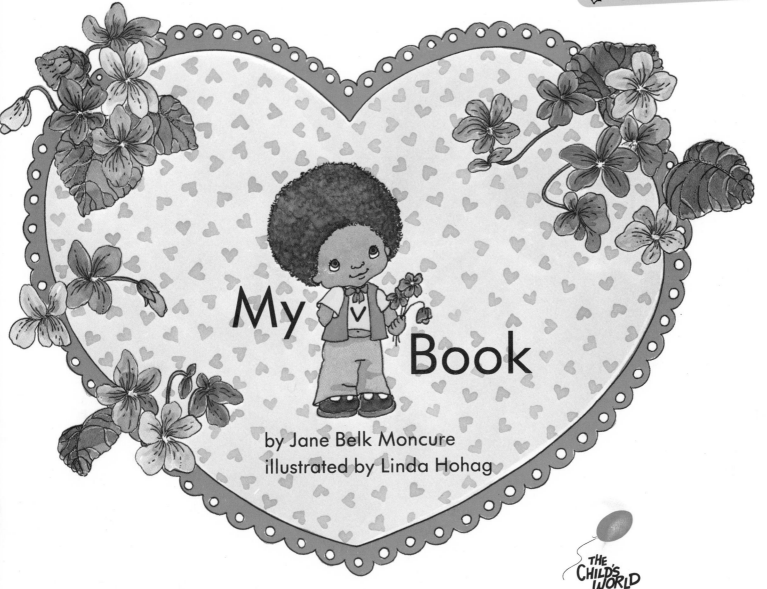

My Book

by Jane Belk Moncure

illustrated by Linda Hohag

THE CHILD'S WORLD

ELGIN, ILLINOIS 60120

Library of Congress Cataloging in Publication Data

Moncure, Jane Belk.
  My "v" book.

  (My first steps to reading)
  Rev. ed. of: My "v" sound box. © 1979.
  Summary: After putting violets, velvet, and a veil in
her box, Little v makes valentines with them and gives
a party.
  1. Children's stories, American.   [1. Alphabet]
I. Hohag, Linda. ill.   II. Moncure, Jane Belk.   My "v"
sound box.   III. Title.   IV. Series: Moncure, Jane Belk.
My first steps to reading.
PZ7.M739Myv 1984   [E]   84-17549
ISBN 0-89565-293-5

Distributed by Childrens Press, 1224 West Van Buren Street,
Chicago, Illinois 60607.

My "v" Book

Little  had a box.

It was a big box.

She said, "I will fill my  box."

She  found violets,

lots of pretty violets.

She put violets 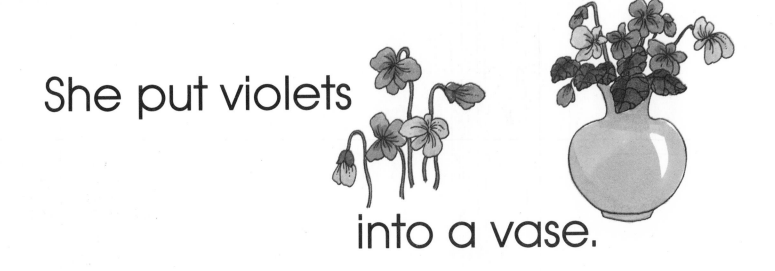 into a vase.

Then she put
the vase
into her box.

Little  found a piece

of velvet,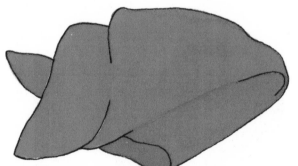

very pretty velvet.

She made a velvet vest.

She put on the vest.

Then she put velvet all around
her box.

Little 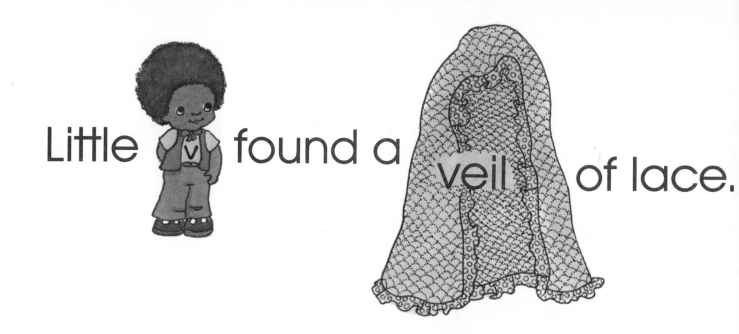 found a veil of lace.

She said, "I can make something with my violets, my velvet, and my veil."

Guess what Little  made?

She made  valentines,

valentines,

valentines.

13

She found a valentine verse.

Roses are red.
Violets are blue.
Sugar is sweet.
So are you!

She wrote the verse on her valentines.

She filled her box with valentines.

She pasted valentines all around it.

But some valentines fell
out of the box.

"I have so many valentines,"
she said.

"I will give them to my friends."

So Little  invited all her

friends to come to a party.

Come to my
party at one,
for Valentine
Day
fun.

She put valentine notes into envelopes. She put names on the envelopes.

What else did she do?

Little  got into her van
and drove to the
mailbox.

Then Little  cleaned the house

with the vacuum cleaner.

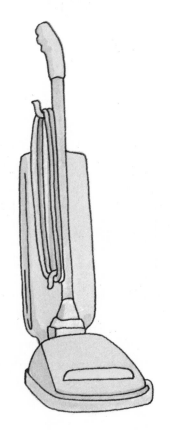

"The vacuum cleaner will clean up this mess," she said.

At last it was time for the valentine party.

All her friends came. They brought valentines.

Little  and her friends made valentine hats.

What pretty valentine hats they made.

Then they opened the valentines.

valentine hats

velvet vest

violets

FEBRUARY

					1	2
3	4	5	6	7	8	9
10	11	12	13	14	15	16
17	18	19	20	21	22	23
24	25	26	27	28		

Happy Valentine's Day

vase

valentine cake

What fun they had

valentine hats

valentine box

velvet runner

at the valentine party.

More words with Little

violin

vegetables

volleyball

vine

volcano

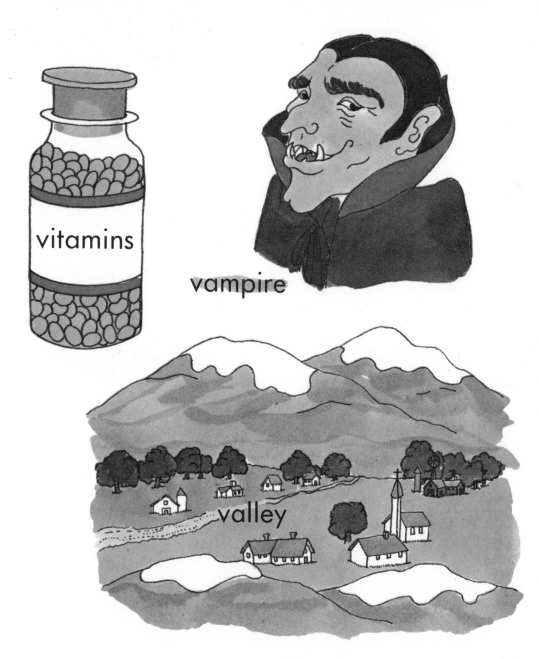

vitamins

vampire

vinegar

valley